THE Cat WANTS Kittens

This is NOT happening.

by **P. Crumble**
Pictures by
Lucinda Gifford

Scholastic Inc.

All rights reserved. Published by Scholastic Inc., *Publishers since 1920.* SCHOLASTIC
and associated logos are trademarks and/or registered trademarks of Scholastic Inc.

The Cat Wants Kittens was originally published in 2018 by
Scholastic Australia, part of the Scholastic Group.

Library of Congress Cataloging-in-Publication Data available

ISBN 978-1-338-74123-0

10 9 8 7 6 5 4 3 2 1   22 23 24 25 26

Printed in China
This edition first printing, January 2022

The text type was set in Granjon and Noyh A Bistro.

To AR and Alex for being the best company ever — PC

For my fellow kittens: Samantha and Robert — LG

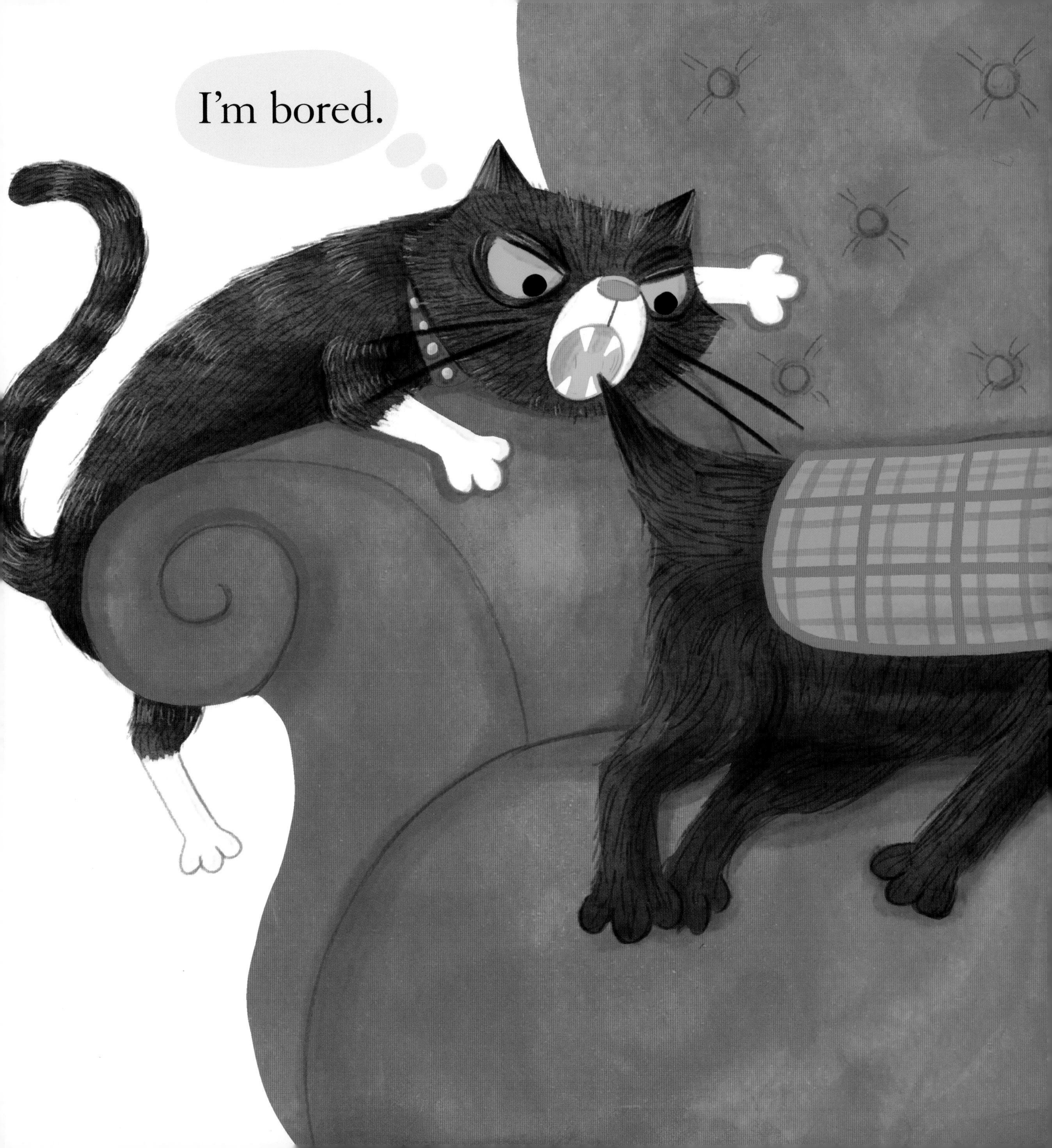
I'm bored.

Perhaps you can fetch...

the Queen of England?
We can catch up
over a cup of tea.

Maybe...

that chef
from TV? She can
cook me a feast.

No?

How about...
a hair stylist. I could
use a new look.

Kevin, we thought you'd enjoy the company of . . .

. . . some new **playmates.**

You thought **wrong**.
I'd rather visit the vet.

I need a little
snack to handle
my nerves.

Yuck!
These furry beasts have no table manners.
I need to work off some stress.

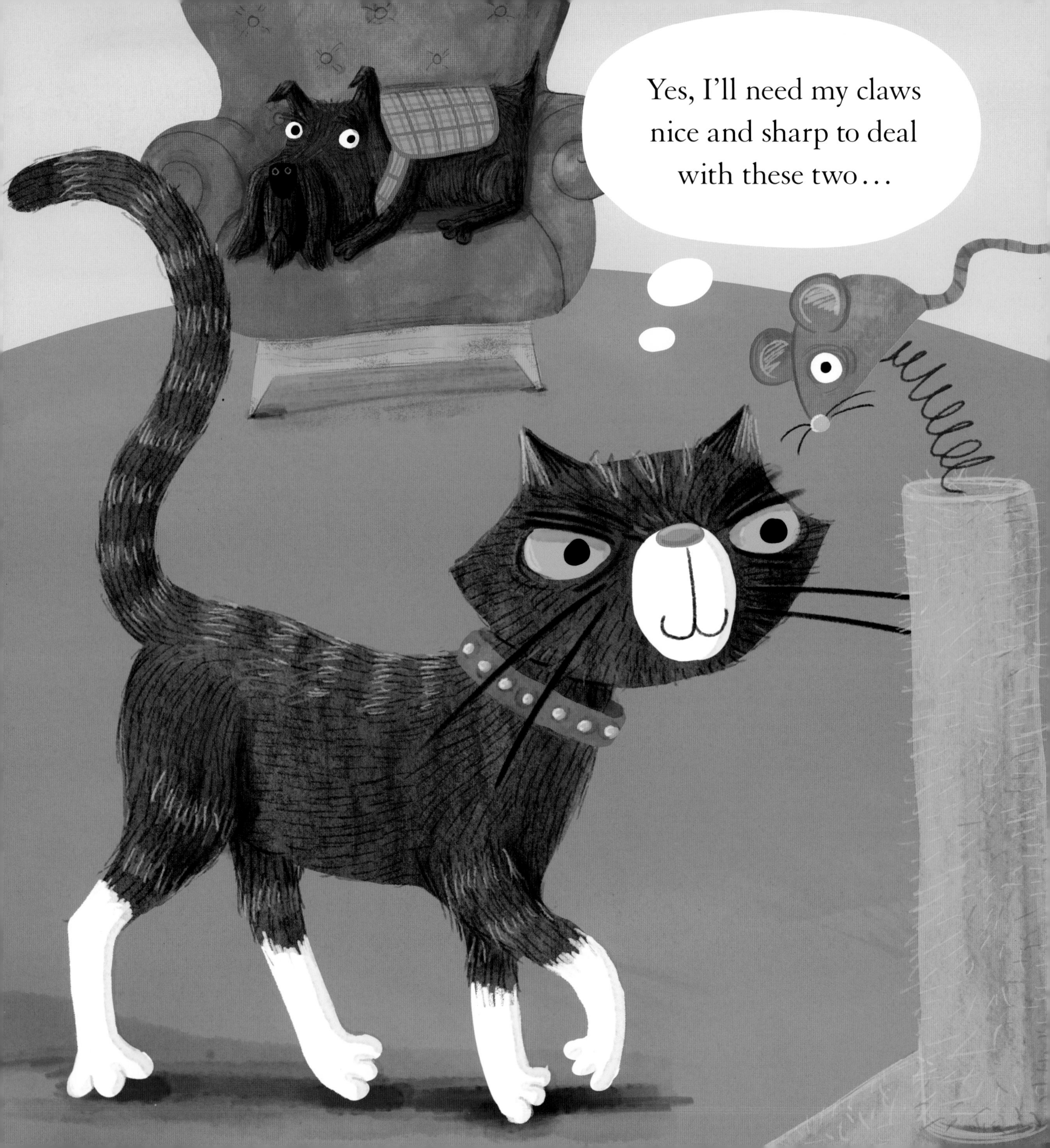
Yes, I'll need my claws nice and sharp to deal with these two…

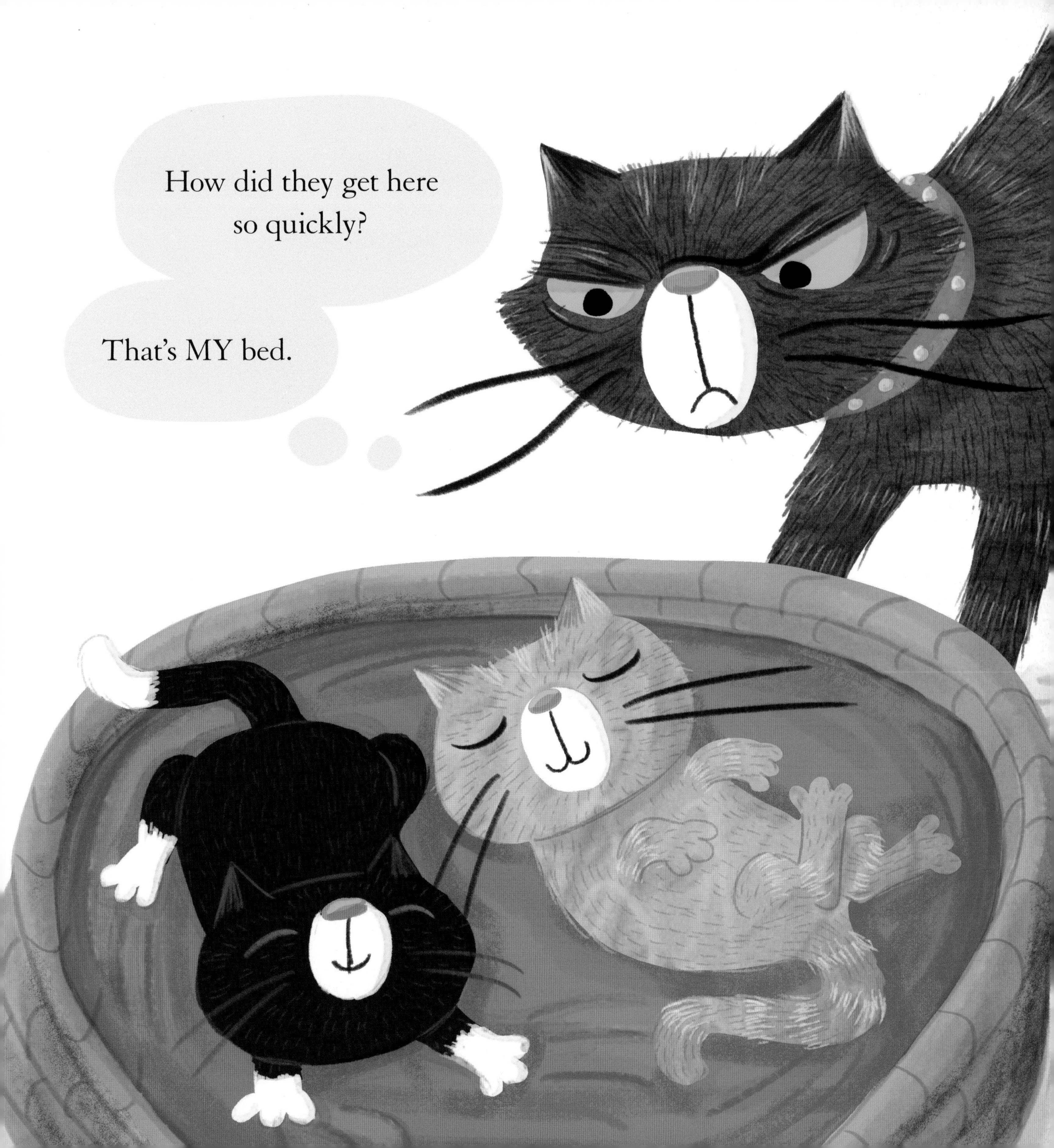
How did they get here so quickly?
That's MY bed.

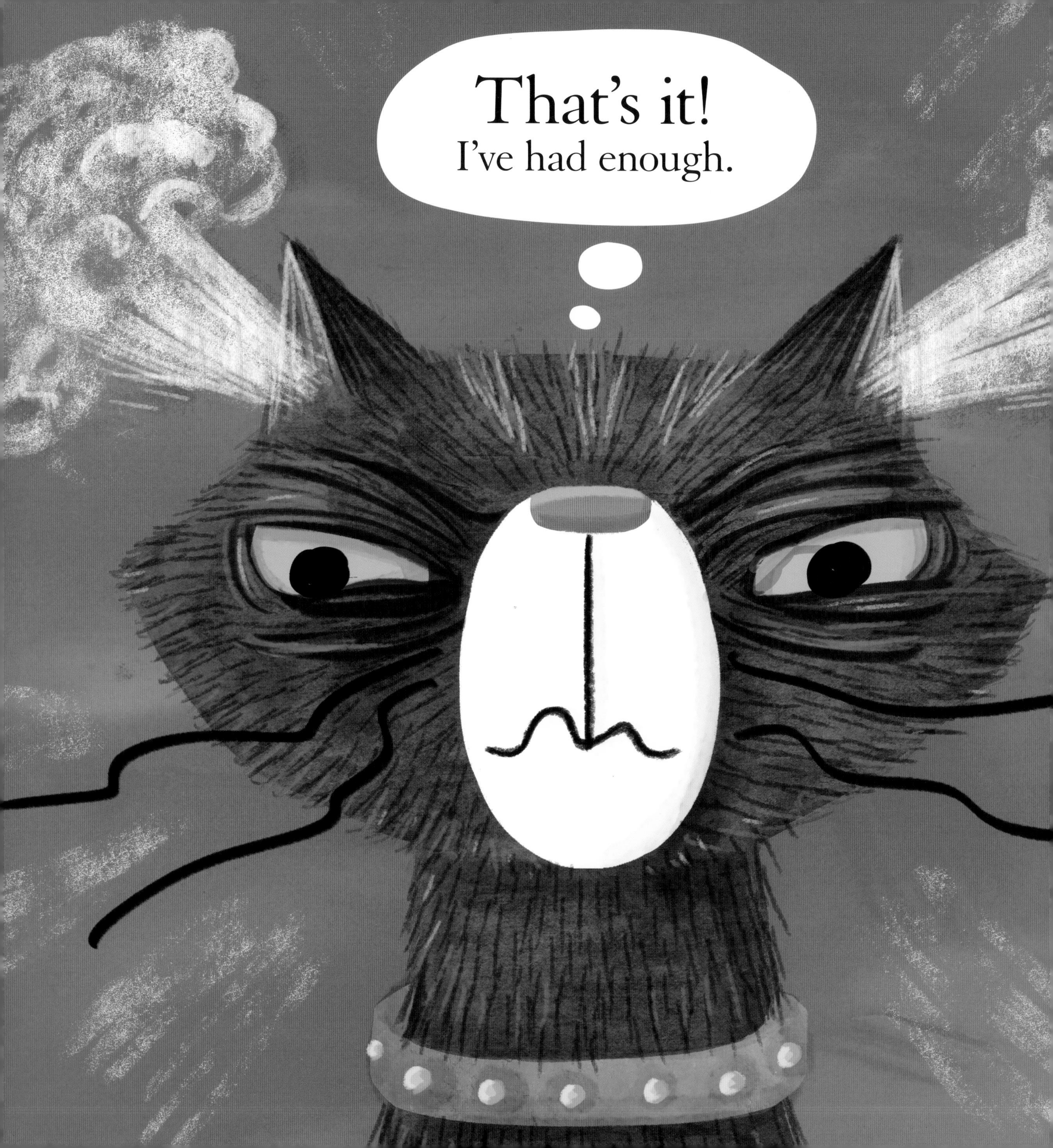
That's it!
I've had enough.

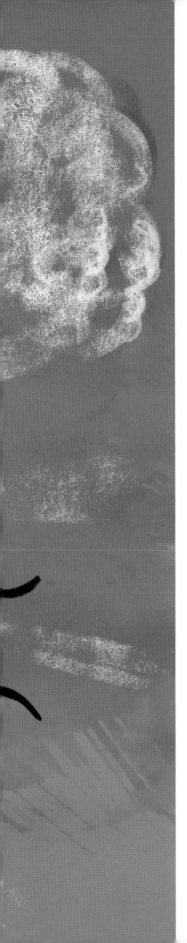

You've left me with
no other choice.

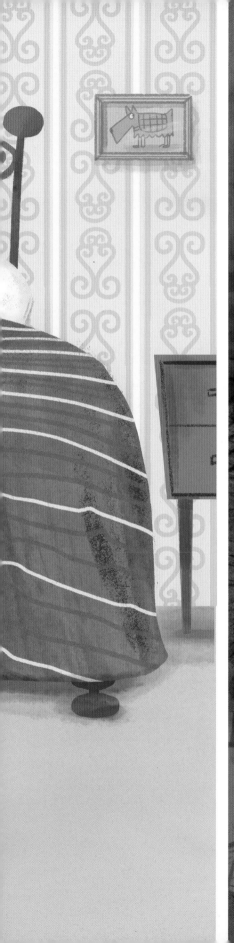

It may be dusty.

The floor may be hard…

…But I'm going to stay here until those pests go away.

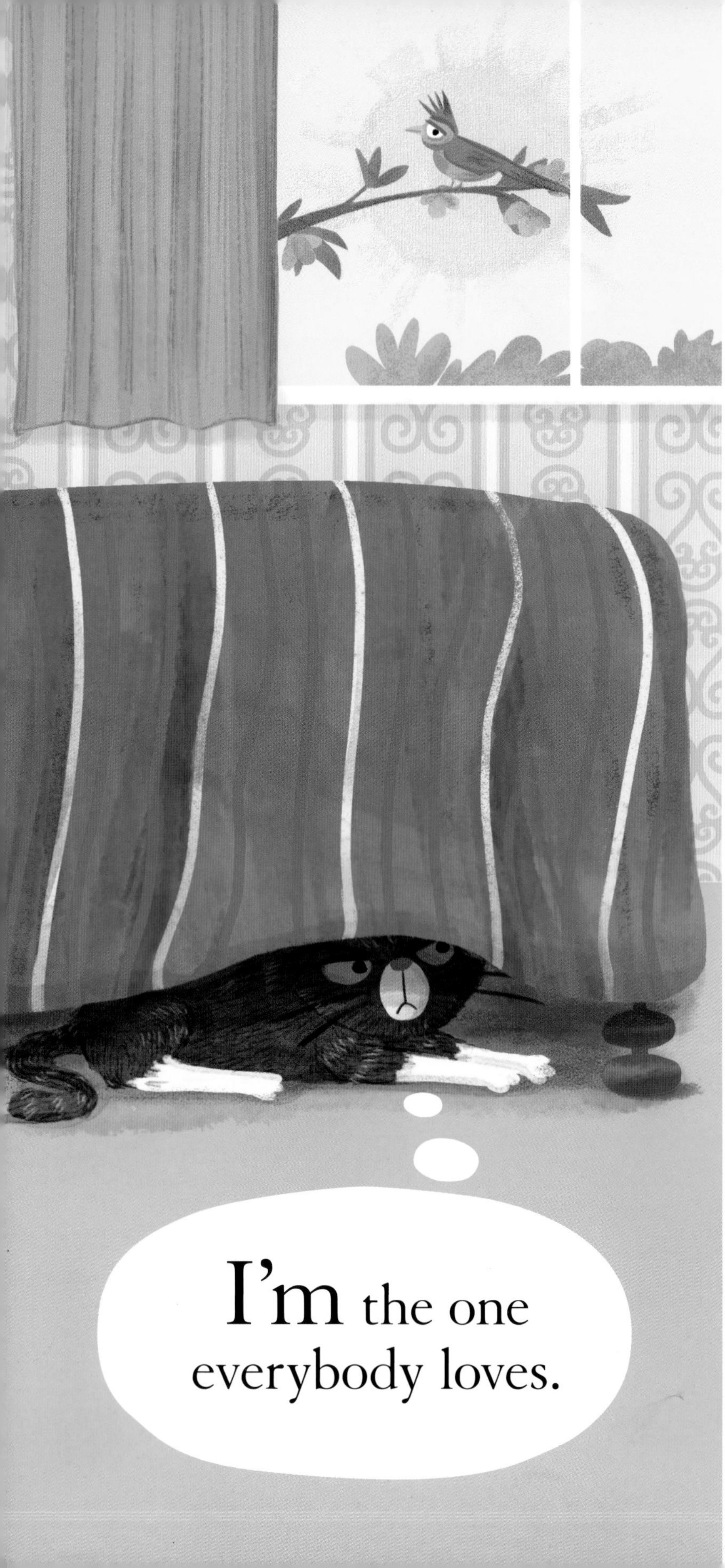
I'm the one everybody loves.

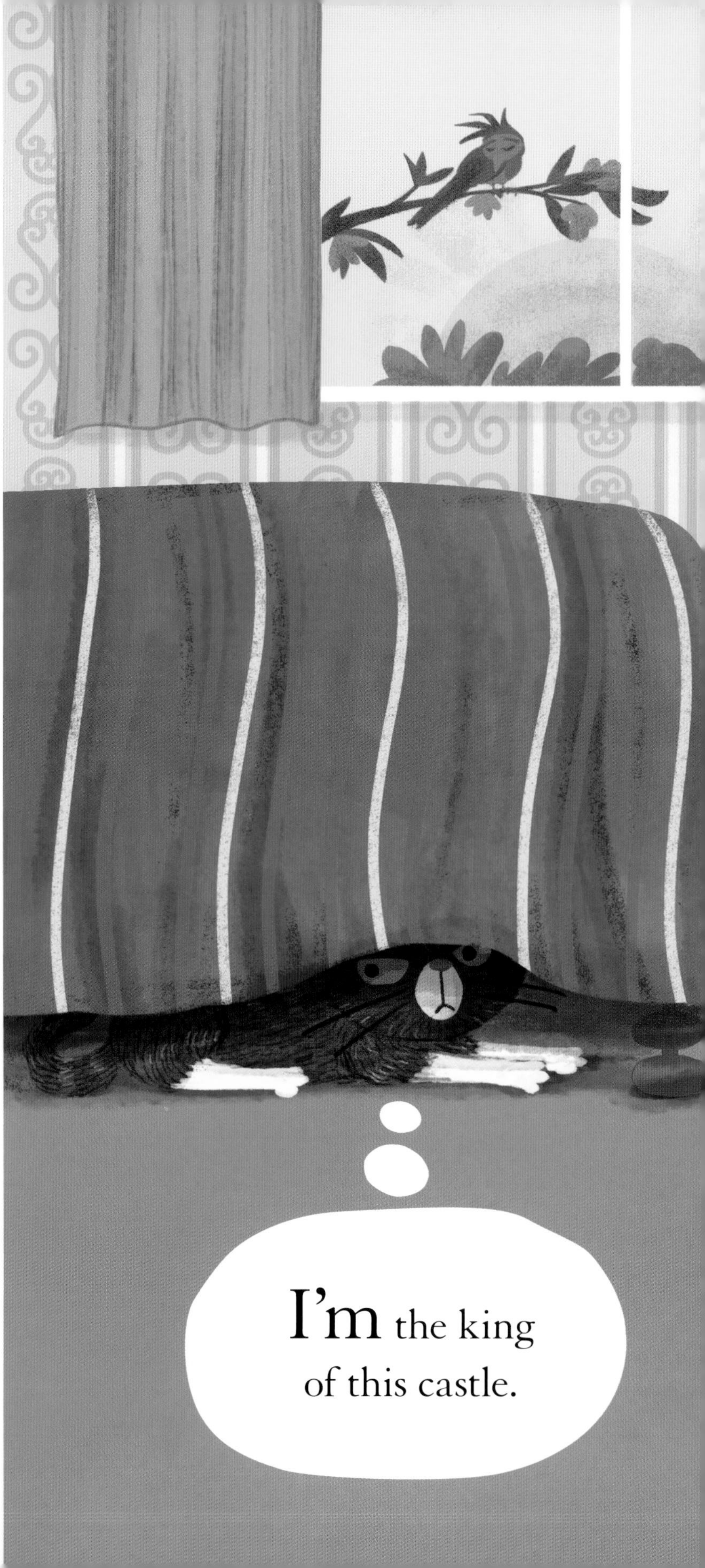
I'm the king of this castle.

Any minute now
they'll come looking
for me.

Wait!

Has everyone
gone to bed?

Well, this is a fine mess.
It looks like I'll have to sort it out myself.

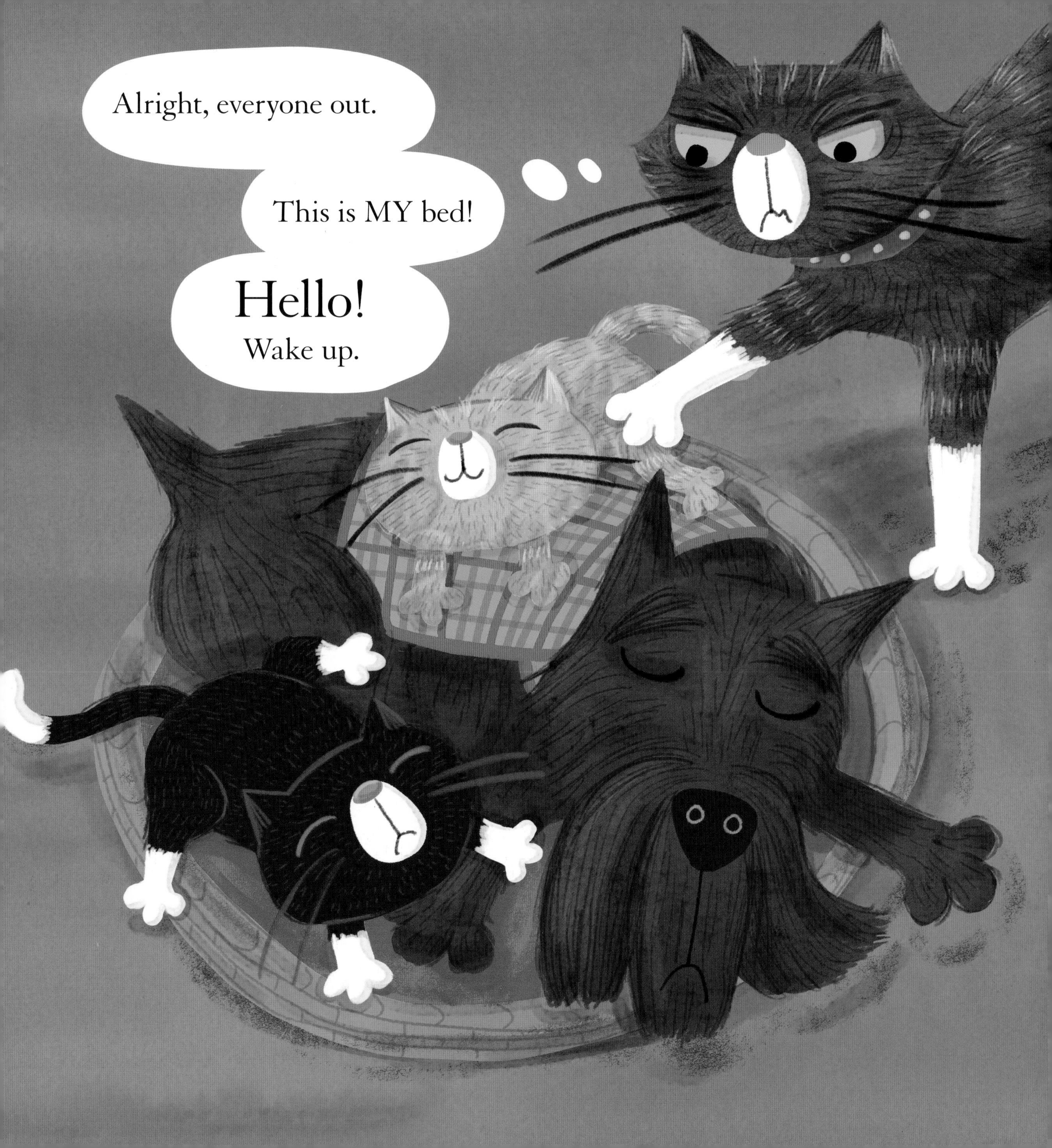
Alright, everyone out.
This is MY bed!
Hello!
Wake up.

Well, I showed them who's boss.